My VILLAINTINE

T.M. FRAZIER
SKYE WARREN
CALLIE HART
SHARI SLADE
LILI ST. GERMAIN

My Sweet Villaintine
Copyright © 2017 by Lili St. Germain, Shari Slade, Skye Warren, Callie Hart, T.M. Frazier

ISBN-13: 978-1543122305
ISBN-10: 1543122302

All rights reserved. Without limiting the rights under copyright reserved above, no part of this publication may be reproduced, stored in or introduced into retrieval system, or transmitted, in any form, or by any means (electronic, mechanical, photocopying, recording, or otherwise) without the prior written permission of both the copyright owner and the above publisher of this book.

This is a work of fiction. Names, characters, places, brands, media, and incidents are either the products of the author's imagination or are used fictitiously. The author acknowledges the trademarked status and trademark owners of various products referenced in this work of fiction, which have been used without permission. The publication/use of these trademarks is not authorized, associated with, or sponsored by the trademark owners.

Cover Designer: Hang Le
Formatting: Champagne Formats

FOREWORD

Get cozy with a villain this Valentine's Day.

FLOWERS OPTIONAL.

To celebrate this Valentine's Day, five of the most twisted minds in dark romance decided to get together and let their demons run wild…

Each author has brought something unique to the table - or should we say, some*ONE*. A terrifying villain. A broken antihero. A sexy bad boy.

Why isn't this available to purchase on retailers like Amazon or iBooks?

Simple - because we knew we wanted to break ALL the rules. We wanted to bring you the darkest, most fucked-up pieces of our characters. Think dubious consent. Think bondage. Think violent delights. Think "this book is banned" within about an hour.

We didn't want to get banned, yo.

But we DID want to swim in the dark depths of our souls. And you know - for such a dark place, the water is surprisingly warm.

Ready to dip a toe in?

Right this way…

WARNING:
BEYOND HERE LIES DARKNESS

This is not for the faint-hearted.

<u>Proceed at your own risk.</u>

Be prepared to have your heart shattered and your e-reader melting by the time you reach the end of this exclusive dark romance collection.

Orchard

by Skye Warren

THE GIRL NOTICES ME WHEN I WALK IN THE door, heralded by the sad chime of a cracked bell. The stiffness of her spine betrays her. I don't think she recognizes me. If she did she'd slip out the back door, Mary Janes slapping the pavement as she ran home. But she recognizes power.

I take a seat in the corner, sinking onto a vinyl bench with the stuffing peeking out of the seams. The Italian shoes I'm wearing could buy out the mortgage on this godforsaken diner, but no one else wants it. The same way a farmer can look at a dry plot of land, I see possibility.

And the ripest fruit is the girl, her cheeks pink

from exertion, wisps of blond hair curling over her temple. Every man in this place watches her as she bustles and sweats to earn every two-dollar tip. It's the closest they come to making her stroke their cocks, having her fetch watered-down coffee, again and again.

She breezes over, mug and pot in hand, pouring before I've ordered. "What can I get you?"

I nod toward the glass platter on the counter. "What kind of pie?"

"Peach."

Of course. "I'll have that."

She manages a brief smile, not quite meeting my eyes, before bustling back to get me a slice.

Yes, I can see why this derelict diner stays open in the war zone that is west Tanglewood. If I only had ten dollars in my pocket, I wouldn't buy a blow job from the whore on the corner. I'd make this girl scurry back and forth, back and forth.

I have much more than ten dollars to my name.

And she will do a lot more to earn it.

She returns with a slice on a white ceramic plate and a fork. It's obscene, the way the fruit has slid from the cuts, the glisten of sweet syrup. The way strips of flesh-colored crust drape over the filling.

"What's your name?"

She hesitates only a moment. "Penny."

Her full name is Penelope Margaret Hartford. Such a dignified name for a baby born addicted to drugs from her bitch of a mother, her father in prison before she drew her first ragged breath. "How long have you been working here, Penny?"

She hesitates a little longer this time. Eventually she'll give me everything—her body, her sanity. But I want to see how far I can push first.

"Two years."

Two years would have made her fifteen years old. I've owned Mel's Diner since before that, but I never came here. Never saw her. And that's a damn shame. How sweet would it have been to see her cheeks rounded with youth, her knees knobby?

Fifteen would have made her underage for what I have planned. That's also a damn shame. I prefer to break every rule that exists, prefer anarchy to order. I would have fucked her peachy little cunt when she was underage. Illegal. Naturally, I'll still do it. A little more coercion, a little more twisted desire, will make her just as delicious.

I tip my head toward the cup of coffee, exactly where she left it before. "I prefer two creams. Three sugars."

She pauses, uncertain whether to shove the

small container of watery creams and old sugar toward me. That's what a busy diner waitress would do for a normal customer, but I'm far from normal.

In fact, I don't prefer this weak excuse for coffee at all, but I want to see her dither. I want to see her weigh whatever tip this rich stranger might give against the gas bill at home, weigh her natural desire to obey against the sexual undertone of my request.

After a moment, she reaches for the ceramic container. Slender fingers dig out two tiny cups of cream. Three paper packets of sugar. Her hands are shaking as she pours them into the mug.

White nondairy creamer swirls into the center, embraced by the black. Sugar sinks to the bottom.

I make no move to hold the spoon, to stir them into the coffee. There's a surface kind of strength that men seek—always controlling with their hands, their bodies. Even their words. God, the sweet pressure around my cock as she obeys me without a single sound, as she rushes to please me without my even issuing a command. It's inherent between us, my authority, her obeisance. She can feel it, even if she doesn't understand it.

She picks up the spoon and stirs until the coffee becomes a warm brown, swirling around silver.

"Is that—" She catches herself, wondering why she's doing this for me, most likely. Wondering what hold I have over her. "Is that everything?"

Not even close. "What time do you get off?"

How many times has someone asked her this? If a man is young and handsome, it means he's asking her on a date. I'm betting plenty have tried. I'm not young. At least twenty-five years her senior. And I'm definitely not handsome. The last escort I fucked said I look like the devil himself. She had my fingerprints bruised on her neck, so that might have influenced her opinion.

A small shake of her head, almost as if she's gathering herself. "That's not really—"

"Appropriate? I'm rarely appropriate."

"I'll come back and check on you in a little bit."

"I'd rather you sit down with me."

She takes a step back. "Please stop."

What a good girl, protecting herself. Too bad it won't help.

I watch as she ducks into the kitchen. Checking on a meal, or hiding from me? When she emerges, she avoids my side of the diner completely, delivering food and handing out checks without making eye contact. Such a little press into her boundaries, such a lovely display of vulnerability. There's so much more for us to explore.

I drop a hundred-dollar bill on the table, leaving the coffee and the pie untouched. She'll think about me for the rest of her shift. For the rest of the week. She'll look over her shoulder for me.

I'm a farmer in this concrete land, money my tool, fear a steady fall of rain.

And very soon, I'll pick the sweetest peach for myself.

Darkness coats the city like sweet dew, nourishing and slick. It's my favorite time to walk the streets, when no one recognizes me. Unless I want them to.

I'm six steps behind little Penny, cloaked in shadow. She knows someone follows her, but she doesn't know who. Does my face come to mind— silver eyes and black hair? Does she know which wolf stalks her? On the west side of Tanglewood, it could be a nameless rapist. Not Jonathan Scott, the amoral businessman who owns most of this cracked concrete.

My footsteps echo off the bricks on either side.

She speeds up, her shoes slapping the wet

pavement. Her shoulders hunch down, instinctively making her smaller. She's already so petite, body thin and undernourished. Except for her tits and ass, a red flag to bulls like me. Her body can't help but be fertile. She can't help but attract me.

Poor Penny. She can't help being so fun to break.

Around the corner toward her house, she spurs into a run. My steps lengthen to their usual stride, but I don't chase after her. Not quickly. Not when she's running straight into the trap I've set. The entire tenement is a maze made for small people, powerless people.

Her door is shut, the lock turned.

I knock. There's a key in my pocket the property manager gave me. I'd rather be let inside. The devil wants an invitation.

The door opens a crack, yanked short by a brass chain. A wide, fearful brown eye takes me in. "You."

"Me," I say agreeably. "May I come inside?"

"Who are you?"

The man who's going to strip you down, layer by layer. Until I get to your beating heart. "The owner of this building."

Her eyes narrow. "You're not the super."

"He works for me."

"How do I know I can trust you?"

My cock twitches at being challenged, even this small amount. My reputation is so absolute, my power so replete that I rarely find this—especially from a girl so small.

"You definitely can't trust me. Run and tell your daddy that Jonathan Scott is here."

She shuts the door and turns the deadbolt with a squeak. I hear soft voices through the thin walls but not what they're saying. I can imagine it well enough. *Jonathan Scott? Are you serious? Open the fucking door. Let him in before he kicks it in.*

I would never do something so crass. I became powerful so that I could direct people instead of the other way around. The door opens about sixty seconds later.

A breathless Penny swings open the door. "Come in."

An older man hobbles inside, leaning on both the wall and a single crutch. His leg is wrapped in denim, a poor man's cast. Someone who can't afford health care. "Mr. Scott," he says, cheeks ruddy, eyes bright with pain and fear. "What can we do for you?"

"Please sit down, George. Don't strain yourself

on my account."

He hesitates, clearly preferring to stand even as his balance wavers. No one wants to sit down around an animal baring its teeth. Penny helps him to a lumpy plaid armchair. Such a good daughter.

I do him the favor of sitting across from him, on an old corduroy sofa. It's a courtesy I can extend since I'll have my cock in his daughter tonight. "I understand my son has been to visit you."

Fear glistens over the man's eyes. He glances at his broken leg. "I told him we'd get it. I swear."

I shake my head, disappointed. "Don't lie to me. There's no way for you to get ten thousand dollars. Little Penny could serve a hundred pies a day, and you'd never be able to pay."

"Stop it," Penny says, brown eyes flashing. "Leave him alone."

Like biting into a peach, the slight crisp, the hint of tartness beneath the sweetness. Heat courses through my body, rare for someone so jaded, so fucking experienced. Almost an old man, really.

"I could," I say idly. "Leave him alone, I mean. If you want me to."

A hard swallow. "What do you mean?"

"Ten thousand dollars." I pull out an envelope

thick with hundred dollar bills. Just like the one I left her on the Formica table in the diner. I cock my head, studying her. "Would you like this, Penny?"

George looks concerned. "No, leave her out of this. She didn't have nothing to do with it."

"You'll have to give the money to Damon yourself. Do you think you could manage that? Or would you gamble again, hoping to turn it into twenty or thirty thousand?"

"I'll make sure he gets it," Penny says with a worried glance at her daddy.

"You won't."

She doesn't want to ask. She has no choice. "Why not?"

"You'll be with me."

"No!" George says, struggling to heave himself up. An involuntary sound of pain fills the cramped apartment as he leans too much on his leg. "You can't do this."

He knows it's already done. He should have known that when I showed up at the door. Maybe he did. Maybe he sent his little girl to the door knowing it would be the last time.

"It's up to you," I say, smiling at her.

An impossible choice. A dirty old man with a

taste for sweetness. Her lips firm. "You're a monster."

Fuck, I almost come in my pants. "That's right," I murmur. "Fight me."

"How dare you do this?"

"Offer you money? Well, sure, call the cops. Tell them how horrible I am for paying your daddy's debts."

"Aren't the police in your pockets?"

"Or you can take your chances with Damon Scott. He has quite a reputation." I glance at George's leg. "I suppose you're already familiar with it. What did he promise to take next?"

A furtive glance at his daughter is the only answer I need. Damon is my son, after all.

"Tick tock," I say softly. "Would you like the money?"

She looks to her daddy in that trusting, hopeful way a child does. Of course, her father has no comfort to offer. He can't even meet her eyes. That's the way Damon looked at me once. I didn't comfort him either.

"I'll do it," she says between clenched teeth.

I stand and leave the room without another word. The money remains on the cheap cushion where I left it. Her footsteps chase me down the hallway.

"Wait." She's breathless. "I'm coming."

I beat her down the uneven stairs and into the night. Only on the street do I let her catch up. "I don't wait for you, little girl. That's not how this works."

She bites her lip, clearly holding back some retort. The fire in her burns, where for too many years I felt numb. "Okay. I'll be good. I swear."

"Do you really think Daddy is going to use the money to pay off the debt?"

Large brown eyes look up at the building behind me. That's the true monster, its bones rotting wood, its skin crumbling concrete. Glassy eyes stare out, unblinking as it eats people up. There's no way her father will give the money to Damon. He'll gamble it away, ending up in more debt. It's a sickness.

The glimmer of hope in her eyes is a stroke to my cock.

"He knows what I'm giving up."

"Do you?"

Her eyes narrow, fierce with righteous anger. "You want to have sex with me."

"Wrong."

Even she knows that will be worse. Suspicion. Fear she tries to hide. "What, then?"

"I want to break you down into parts—into hope and despair. Into love and fear. I want to consume your humanity, feast on you, until there's nothing left but a small, jagged core at the center."

She should be afraid, and she is. More than that, she's defiant.

I knew I chose the best piece.

"Why?"

I laugh softly. "Do you ever think about how mechanical sex is? Men so desperate for something warm and wet to fuck. A purely physical sensation. We might as well be automatons."

"Not you," she says with a hint of bitterness.

It would be better if I only wanted to rape her. She knows that much.

"I learned to block out physical sensations as a child." I believe in honesty, in exposure. Secrets are weakness. "Pain. Sex. Hunger. They only touch our bodies. Not our minds."

She looks horrified. "What happened to you?"

I hold out my hand. "Come along."

It may as well be a snake, my fingers its fangs. "You're insane."

"No, little peach. I'm the only sane one in a world full of rabid animals." I have endless patience as I leave my hand outstretched. Mercy is important. Mercy to a girl who'll be broken soon enough.

She trembles as she puts her palm against mine.

I squeeze in comfort. I'm not a heartless man.

We take a long walk through the back alleys of the west side. Five blocks south and two west. The sign for the Midtown Asylum has long since crumbled, leaving only a large, plantation-style building. If the west side of Tanglewood is my orchard, then this building is the barrel of bruised fruit. It will be mashed and strained. Still useful for its indelible flavor, but no longer bearing the same colors.

On either side, there are houses falling down. I could repair them. Or maybe rent them as they are, to people desperate enough for a leaky roof. But I prefer the privacy. There's no one else on this street.

I have mansions and compounds scattered across Tanglewood, shows of wealth and of strength. They're fine for me to visit, to use like a simple man fucks a slick cunt. Temporary relief.

This is the only place I ever feel human.

I hear her indrawn breath before the lock has turned.

Pictures spread over the floor. The insides of senators' houses. The interiors of city hall. Windows into our twisted little world. I haven't hidden any of them from her—like I said, I believe in honesty.

"The desk," I tell her, hanging my coat on a hook.

She takes a step forward. A soft moan of denial. "You watched me."

Her little bedroom with its faded quilt. The place she peeled off her cheap waitress uniform. The bed she slept in. "Sometimes at night, I'd hear you breathe faster. See your hand moving under the covers. It's so beautiful, the way you love yourself."

Her eyes are wide. Expression solemn. "I'm not leaving here, am I?"

"Not alive." Maybe she'd be breathing. Maybe she wouldn't.

Her mind would be cracked beyond repair.

It's inevitable that she would run, like a hand shrinking back from fire. She sprints for the door, her hand on the knob before I catch her slender body in my arms. It's a thrill to toss her onto the ground, to climb on top of her back. I do love when they run. That's the animal side of me. Sometimes I'm feral too.

The difference is I have a bigger goal. A better one.

I stroke her cheek with the backs of my fingers.

"Lovely peach. So sweet."

She fights me, thrashing on the ground. Beating the concrete with her fists. "You're disgusting."

"Yes," I breathe. "You see it now. It's hard wearing suits. Wearing authority and power. The way people look at me—reverence. Fear. Not you."

It only takes a moment to open my pants, to push up the thin fabric of her skirt. To pull aside her panties. My cock notches against her puckered hole, and she freezes. "Wait," she says. "Wait, wait, wait."

"That's right," I whisper. "Beg."

Hands clench into fists. All that courage. "Don't do it. Not like this."

"On the floor. Held down like an animal. Looking at the face of the man you'll grow to love." I may taste her first, but she's a gift. A gesture of paternal love. The sweetest fruit for the very best son.

Damon looks so much like me. Younger, of course. Kinder.

My face will haunt her nightmares. She'll be terrified of him. That's my gift to him—her fear.

I plunge into her, ripping a scream from her throat. Her back muscles spasm around my cock, stretching and fighting the intrusion. My cock aches from entering her dry. What bliss. I press my face against the top of her head and breathe deep. She still smells like grease and stale coffee from the diner. Perfect.

From the side, I can see her face scrunched in pain. Tears leak down her cheeks.

"Watch," I say, nudging deeper with my cock. Did she think this was as hard as I could fuck her? I'm showing tenderness now. She glances back at me, still subsumed with the physical pain.

I reach to my back pocket and pull out my phone. It only takes a few clicks. The feed pulls up on the screen. There's her father, blowing the ten thousand dollars on useless bets.

Her sob fills my ears, a sweeter music than grunts and groans ever could be.

"You'll save that little cunt for someone special," I whisper into her ear. "Someone you love as much as me. I won't fuck you there."

"I hate you," she whispers, voice thick. In a thick hock, she spits. It lands on the phone screen, glistening and foamy. "I hate you, I hate you."

What she doesn't realize is that it hurts me at first. No lube. No saliva. But as I saw in and out of her, she lubricates with blood. That makes it the best place to fuck a woman. Or a man. A test of character.

Nature's gift to the powerful creatures.

Damon doesn't see that. He still likes to fuck a slick, swollen cunt. He likes to make a woman spasm around his cock—in pleasure instead of pain. That makes him weak, no matter how many legs he breaks. What kind of father would I be if I didn't fix that?

Honestly, she's a mess.

I pull out and grasp my cock, pink and dark from her blood. One stroke, two. I aim toward the gaping hole, bright red and pulsing blood. I pump my cock until milky semen spurts across her pretty ass.

It's almost emotional, looking at her wound in the place I became a man.

I stand and fix my clothes, picking up the phone from where I dropped it. Exposure. I snap a picture of her. A few, because I want to make sure the lighting is just right. I've spent enough time preparing the piece, I should make the most of it.

Then I grasp her by the hair and drag her down a hallway. Third room on the right.

The Recreation room. A pool built for someone who wanted the crazy to exercise. Maybe even have fun. A metal grate lid added to keep people from falling in. It has a different purpose now.

Her feet scrabble for purchase on the broken tiles. She can't fight the pull. Such beautiful blond strands. They look delicate framing her flushed face, but they aren't. They're strong. Like her. A wonderful leash with which to pull her into hell.

The hole gapes in the center of the room, black and dank.

She swings wildly in a punch that lands on my side. A very nice attempt, but not enough. I push her into the pit. The sound of her fall echoes against the walls. Six feet. Far enough to break something. She slips as she tries to stand, the concrete sides slick with mildew.

"Don't worry," I murmur. "This will help you, too."

What if he doesn't come? Then he would be more heartless than I am, and wouldn't that be sweet? A truly proud moment as a father. I think he'll come. He'll hate her. She'll fear him.

I turn the faucet on the wall, and water pours from a small steel pipe into the pit. She screams when she realizes what will happen. It will take a long time, but eventually, the pit will be full of water. The metal grate I slide over the top will keep her inside.

As it rises, she'll have to kick to stay afloat.

Ultimately, she'll cling to the metal grate, her fingers through the holes, desperately sucking in air through the top. And then her arms will tire. Her mind will dull. The heroic Damon Scott will come for her, possibly. He might even come in time.

How long will she survive down there?

What will be left of her mind if she does?

"Please, no," she begs. She's really lovely like this, desperate and clawing.

I almost wish that I could keep her. Almost. "Don't panic," I say, chiding. "You'll only lose your head."

Tears stream down her cheeks. "Don't do this to me. I'll do anything, anything."

"You'll do everything, lovely peach."

"I'll make the money back. Work in the clubs. For sex. Anything. Don't do this to me. *Please.*"

Desperation is an aphrodisiac. I knew that, which was partly why I had to fuck her first. It doesn't stop my cock from growing hard again. "Do you know, when I first got here, they still did lobotomies. How barbaric is that?"

"*This* is barbaric," she half cries, half screams. "Let me out. Oh my God, let me out of here."

The water is already at her knees. "They did many cruel things, but not this. This was beautiful.

I fought it first. That's the weakness inside us. It's a gift to make you stronger."

She backs up in the water, back against the corner, eyes wide with horror.

"Oh, I almost forgot." I pull up the picture on my phone and start a text to Damon. He doesn't have this number. It's one of many burner phones. Anonymous. Untraceable.

On impulse, I add a heart emoji. It makes me smile. He probably doesn't know I know how to use those. His old man. I may be a little traditional, but I can learn. I hit *Send*.

Only a second passes before he calls back.

I shove the phone into my pocket. We don't need to speak. He's my son. Our connection goes deeper than words. He'll know from the picture where she is. After all, this is where I made Damon stronger. The world is a cruel, dark place. I wanted him to be ready for it.

It feels a little melancholy to leave her there, the sweet fruit and the familiar barrel. God, even the smell of antiseptic lingers in the air decades later. I breathe in the scent for comfort.

Strange to realize I want the girl for myself. How I could torment her. In one of my mansions, using every room, every piece of ominous equipment. No clothes. Little food. Those beautiful, large brown eyes, full of fury. She's almost too good for him.

I pause with my hand on the doorknob, looking back down the hallway. Faintly, the water babbles, a peaceful sound like a brook. I'm watering her like a fucking plant. Making her grow.

And isn't that why farmers work so hard? To pass down the land to their sons?

It doesn't matter if I want to keep her. I can still feel the tight muscles of her asshole tearing around my cock. Still feel her hair in my fist. I want to consume her a hundred times. And then again.

My sacrifice doesn't matter.

She serves a bigger purpose—a family legacy.

Thank you for reading Orchard!

Jonathan Scott is a character in the Endgame series, which begins with *The Pawn* and continues in *The Knight*. I hope you'll try this dark + sexy virgin auction series!

"Skye Warren's THE PAWN is a triumph of intrigue, angst, and sensual drama. I was clenching everything. Gabriel and Avery sucked me in from the first few paragraphs and never let go." – New York Times bestselling author Annabel Joseph

"Gabriel Miller is the perfect alpha, leaving you reeling as his dominance, power, and unexpected tenderness creates the ideal mixture. Five glowing stars." - New York Times bestselling author Aleatha Romig

Check out Skye's website at www.skyewarren.com

Turn the page for the next dark tale in this collection,
courtesy of heart-stopper author Callie Hart…

BY CALLIE HART

BLOOD AND CUM: MY BODILY FLUIDS combine together easily in the bottom of the glass tumbler, the liquid a dark crimson mixture when I'm done. The jerking off part was less fun than fucking, I'll admit, but pressing the blade into my flesh and gathering the blood? That part was organic. The way the sharpened steel cut? The way my body bled? My dick stirs, growing hard again just thinking about it. I can't think about that now, though. I have to concentrate. This ritual is important, a ritual the men of our family participate in but once in their lifetimes. I refuse to fuck it up.

Genevieve Kendrick sits on the edge of the

bed, watching me. She's nervous, I can tell, and that only adds to the thrill. She's here of her own volition. She can leave any time she wants, but she won't. We've been going back and forth, playing a cat and mouse game for so long, but she knows the truth just as well as I do: she ran, but she wanted to be caught. She hid, but she wanted to be found. She refused me, but she was always going to surrender herself.

Her long black hair twists in curls over her bare shoulders, almost reaching her hips. Her lips are swollen and red, her skin pale and flawless in the cool, glowing light of the city that floods in through the wide, stain glass windows. The Bastien house is one of the oldest, grandest buildings in the French Quarter of New Orleans. For the past two hundred and fifty-eight years, people have walked by the imposing entrance, choked with Spanish Moss and ivy, and wondered at the architecture—the warm pink stone of the high walls that seems to glow when the sunlight hits it at the right time of day, and the chipped and flaking paint around the expansive windows on each of the three stories. They've thought to themselves, "Such a beautiful building. Such a remarkable place. How luck the people inside must be, to live in a home like that."

If only they knew the reality of it. If only they knew that all who abide inside these four walls are fucking cursed.

The house is the only possible location for tonight's activities, though. No one asks questions when you arrive under the cover of darkness here. No one raises an eyebrow when your guests are screaming out to God at the top of their lungs at three in the morning. Genevieve shifts on the bed, trying to look relaxed, but she's not fooling anybody, least of all me.

"What are you going to do with that?" she asks, eyeing the small glass flask in my hands. She doesn't look scared, per se. Maybe just…curious. Wary and curious. I like the look on her.

"Nothing you won't enjoy," I reply. "Stand up."

Her hands clench into loose fists for a second. She gets to her feet, her long, cream colored silk dress swaying like liquid light around her body, hugging her slender frame and swelling over her curves in the most delicious way. She looks like she could be consumed. Drunk or eaten perhaps, a delicacy only a few men in this world could ever possibly afford. I don't need to pay for luxuries like Genevieve, though. Women like her fall at my feet like I'm some kind of god. All it takes is a rough word, a few carefully chosen commands, the promise of a switch against their bare skin, and they are mine.

She knows about the body in the trunk of my car. She was sitting in the back seat when I met with Farriagamo. She saw him pull a knife on me, and she saw what I did with it when I took it off him. She watched him die, and she watched me drag his limp body from the side of the road and toss it like trash into the trunk of the car. And still…here she sits. Here, she waits for me to make her mine in every sense of the word. This is what it means to be alpha. To have someone completely under your control, no matter how wicked or evil your actions might be.

"Take this." I hold the knife out to Genevieve. The silver of the blade is still covered in the blood and semen I was just mixing together. She stares at it, fixated on the fiercely sharp tip of the weapon where a bead of blood hangs, threatening to fall.

She has three seconds. Three seconds to take the thing before there will be consequences. I think maybe she sees me make this decision, maybe the expression on my face changes, because she jolts into action, crossing the room and taking the knife from me with shaking hands.

"Now what?" she asks.

"Now you lick it clean."

Her eyes grow wide, but she's a smart woman. She knows better than to say anything. To react beyond the quickening of her breath and the dilation of her pupils. Lifting the knife to her mouth, the tip of her tongue darts out between her lips, cautiously, as if she's preparing herself for what comes next, hesitating. I restart the clock.

Three seconds.

One…

Two…

Her tongue runs up the length of the knife. She closes her eyes, a muffled moan catching in the back of her throat as she tastes me.

"That's it. Good girl. Lick it clean." My cock is growing harder by the second. I'm gonna be palming myself soon, stroking the length of my dick, and I'm going to enjoy Genevieve watching me, but for now I'm too wrapped up in her obedience. It's fucking amazing to see her comply without protest like this. The crimson blood on the pale pink of her tongue is driving me insane. When she's finished, she hands me back the knife.

"Open your mouth," I tell her. "Stick out your tongue. Show me." She shows me her tongue. With her head tipped back, her lips pouty and flecked with blood, I want to rip that fucking dress from her body and slam myself inside of her already. I'm a pleasure delayer, though. I like to torture myself a little bit. Make myself wait. "Go back to the bed. Sit on your hands."

Once she's done as I've asked her, I walk over to the door and open it. Jerome stands there, back ramrod straight, hands clasped behind his back, waiting patiently just as I knew he would be. His facial features are impassive as he bows his head slightly, taking a step forward. "He's arrived, sir, as have your brothers. You would like me to escort them to the reception room?"

Excitement shuttles up and down my body, catching me off guard. I'm looking forward to this. I've known all my life that I would have to do this at some point, and the very idea of it was nothing short of inconvenient. I suppose I never really considered the woman I'd be claiming before, though. Now that the moment has arrived and it's Genevieve sitting on the edge of my bed, waiting anxiously like a trapped exotic bird, the situation is far from inconvenient. It's anything but.

"No. Bring them up here. No sense in wasting time."

Jerome bows his head even further, averting his eyes. "Of course." He moves off down the hallway quickly, hands still clasped behind his back. Back inside my room, Genevieve's eyelids flutter when I turn to her. She does her best to sit still but I can tell she's getting antsy. "What now?" she asks.

"Now, you wait patiently. Can you do that?"

"If that's what you want, then yes."

Holy fuck. The fire in her eyes rages; I can see how hard she has to fight to keep her temper under control. It's a beautiful, beautiful thing. Genevieve is a rare kind of woman. She doesn't lean on anyone for help. She never holds her hand out to be steadied. It would kill her to be beholden to anyone. I think that's part of why this whole thing is so fucking perfect. It's her sacrifice, everything she's giving up to hand herself over to me. It must be the hardest thing she's ever had to do, and she's performing wonderfully.

"It *is* what I want," I say. Men don't play poker with me. I perfected the ability to hide my emotions years ago. The gamblers of New Orleans can never tell if I'm bluffing. No tics. No tells. I give nothing away. Right now, though, I'm finding it hard to keep the pleasure from my face. I wonder if my fiery little Genevieve can see how excited she's making me. I catch a glimpse of myself in the vast mirror mounted on the wall beside the bed, and I note the slight curve to my mouth. The faint glimmer of amusement in my eyes. It's subtle. To someone who doesn't know me very well, I'm sure I still look sinister. Perhaps a little…*evil*? I've never been a fan of that word. I don't believe in inherent good, or inherent bad. I believe in people trying to hide their vices and putting on a good show, so others will think them perfect. I believe that some of us choose to embrace the darkness a little too tightly, but at the end of the day there are always snatches of light to be found if a person were to look hard enough. Even within me, believe it or not.

"Lay back now," I command. Genevieve shivers visibly, but she nods, scooting back until her legs are fully resting on the mattress. She lies down flat on her back, her hands laid palm down on the crisp sheets, fingers spread wide like she's trying to steady herself. I take hold of her by the left ankle, raising her leg until it's almost level with my eyes, and then I slowly, carefully unfasten the slender golden strap around her ankle that's holding her stiletto heel on. I slide the shoe from her foot, and then I remove the heel on her right foot, too.

I've never had a thing for feet before. I've

never even thought about them as a sexual part of a female body, but Genevieve's feet are delectable. What would it feel like to suck her toes into my mouth? To run the tip of my tongue along the delicate arch of her sole? Her dress has hitched up to her thighs. In my mind, I'm running my hands roughly up the inside of her legs, and she's gasping, writhing in ecstasy as I trace my fingers higher, higher, higher…

A gentle knock at the door cuts me off there. Genevieve jumps at the sound, sucking in a deep breath. "Would you like something to calm your nerves?" I ask. "Weed? Whiskey? *Cocaine*?"

She shakes her head.

"Okay, then. Stay there." I loosen my tie as I make my way across the room and open the door. I slip the length of silk from my shirt completely and hand it to West as he enters the room. He takes it without question, as if he was expecting it. Vaughn shoots me a reckless, excited grin as he moves past me and into the room behind our brother. The familial resemblance is extremely apparent between Vaughn and West; they're identical, twins born eight minutes apart. They're tall and dark like me but where my eyes are brown, theirs are pale blue, pale as ice, pale as the morning sky in winter after days and days of rain.

"Good to see you." West's voice is tense and low. Under his breath, he says, "He broke Javier's nose. We had to knock him the fuck out just to stop him from smashing the wall down with his fists." He's talking about David Kendrick. David's three years older than Genevieve, and sorely upset about my plans for his sister. Shame I don't give a fuck.

"We'll wake him up as soon as this is over. Is he still going to be able to drive?"

"Yeah. Just about."

Over West's shoulder, I see Vaughn already inspecting Genevieve, pacing around the bed, drinking her in with a fierce, wolf-like hunger. "She's like a midnight rose. All that dark hair. Those ruby red lips. That pale, beautiful skin." Crouching down to one side of the bed, he cocks his head to one side, frowning slightly as he studies Genevieve. "What's your name, pretty one?"

Her eyes dart to me, looking for guidance. What do I want her to do? I give her a sharp nod of my head. "Genevieve," she responds. Her voice waivers, hinting at fear, but she does me proud. She stays exactly where she is on the bed.

"*Genevieve.*" West considers this. "She's different. I can see why you decided to keep her."

"You *know* why I'm keeping her. She's a means to an end."

"Still." He shrugs, still staring at her. "Doesn't hurt that she looks like *that*."

I'm not surprised that he's taken a shine to her. Genevieve is striking, breathtaking in the truest sense of the word, but it's not just her beauty that separates her from other women. It's the way you feel when your gaze meets hers, like you've been shoved from the roof of a very tall building and you're freefalling toward infinity. It feels as though she holds your soul in the palm of her hand when her focus is on you, and it's a strange, unsettling sensation that leaves you raw and energized at the same time. She has no idea that she holds such power within that gaze of hers. If she did, this situation might easily be reversed. I might be the one laid out on the bed, obedient and ready to serve.

Both West and Vaughn are dressed in black: black jeans, black shirt, black leather jackets. Their black and white Chuck Taylors are equally scuffed and dirty. Hardly suitable attire for this event, but then again this is all very last minute. West moves to the other side of the bed and crouches in the same way that Vaughn did, so that both of them are admiring Genevieve from either side. "She's magnificent," he whispers. Genevieve glances between the two men, only a flicker of surprise registering on her face as she realizes that they're almost impossible to tell apart.

"Alexander?"

Father Gustavo is hovering in the doorway. He *is* appropriately dressed, which is reassuring. He's here, ready and willing to do his duty—very convenient since breaking into the rectory behind the Santa Maria Church and forcing him over here at gun point would have taken time I don't have. He looks wired, wide awake, his salt and pepper hair combed neatly back from his face. His cassock is spotless, brushing the floor, and the huge pectoral cross hanging like a yolk around his neck looks like it's been polished especially for the occasion.

"I wasn't expecting to have to do this for you, Alex," he says gravely. "At least, not quite so unexpectedly."

"Yes, well. When you know, you know, right?" My voice is dripping with sarcasm, and the priest hears it. He blinks, like he has something in his eye, and then he turns his attention to Genevieve.

"The Kendrick girl," he observes. "Do her brothers know about this?"

"One of them. The other will soon enough."

He shoots me a scathing sideways glance. "You're inviting trouble to your doorstep, you realize."

"I'm not inviting it. I'm *demanding* it," I correct him. "You know how I feel about debts, Gustavo. A debt must always be paid. Tommy Hendrick has owed me his pound of flesh for far too fucking long."

Gustavo rolls his eyes. "Must you really…?"

It's laughable that he objects to my language, given what he's about to do for me. I give him a tight-lipped smile. "Let's just get this over with."

"As you wish."

Genevieve shivers as I move and stand at the end of the bed. I hold out my hand to her, and her cheeks seem to grow redder. She takes my hand and allows me to help her up from the bed. West and Vaughn both move to stand on either side of her, looking to me, waiting me to give an order to restrain her, but I shake my head.

"We don't need to use force, do we, Genevieve? You're going to behave. You're going to do as you're told, aren't you?"

Her lips part, her eyes flickering with defiance, but after a second she nods. "You keep your promises. I keep mine. I'll do as you ask."

Poor, poor girl. She doesn't see it yet. This will not be an arrangement of convenience. Yes, she's agreed to my terms in order to save her brother David's life, but I won't be satisfied with that. They say the sins of the father are visited upon the heads of his children. Well, Tommy Kendrick's sins are about to be visited upon his siblings, his sins are about to obliterate their lives, and I intend to enjoy every last second of it. I want payback, and there is no sweeter way of achieving my revenge than actually making Genevieve fall in love with me.

"You're here willingly, yes?" Gustavo asks quietly. He shifts nervously from one foot to another, his gaze flitting from West to Vaughn, avoiding me altogether. Genevieve looks at the priest like he's gone mad.

"*Willingly?*" She sounds like she's about to burst into laughter or tears, one of the two.

"I need to hear you say it," Gustavo says.

A blanket of silence fills the room. We all know what happens if Genevieve suddenly decides she wants to back out of this: West pulls a gun on the priest, and I make her wish she'd never been born. She stands very, very still, looking at me as if she's trying to pick me apart, searching for the thread she needs to tease at to unravel me. To understand me. She sounds frustrated when she finally answers him. "Yes. I am here willingly."

Gustavo breathes a sigh of relief. "Good, good. This is good. Then we'll begin. In the presence of these two witnesses…" He rambles on, talking of god and of commitment. I meet Genevieve's gaze, and I begin to make plans. I don't have time to move slowly. I will figure out how to crack that hard veneer of hers, and I will work out what makes her tick. She's complicated. Perhaps more complicated than any other woman I've met, but still… I'm Alexander Bastien. I will win her heart without a fucking doubt, and when I do…

"Do you, Alexander Frederic Bastien, take this woman, Genevieve Louisa Eleanor Kenrick, to be your wife? Do you promise to be true to her, in good times and in bad. In sickness and in health? Do you promise to love and honor her all the days of her life?"

Ah, the irony. Gustavo knows *I'm* incapable of love. He told my father he thought I was a sociopath when I was just five years old. Asking if I promise to love Genevieve is like asking the sun not to rise. It goes against the laws of physics, of logic, common sense, and any other law you might care to come up with. I know a thing or two about honor, though. "I do," I say. My voice has a hard, stone-worn edge to it. My agreement to Gustavo's question is more than that; it's a threat. Genevieve will be mine forever. There's no way out for her once this is over. She will belong to me no matter what. She must hear this in voice. She goes paler and paler by the second as Father Gustavo asks her the same questions he just asked of me.

"...sickness and in health. Do you promise to love and honor him all the days of his life?"

She swallows. Her pupils look blown, so wide and black that for a brief moment her irises look entirely black. "I do," she whispers.

"Then I now pronounce you man and wife." Gustavo hesitates for a second, and then adds, "May God have mercy on your soul, young lady."

The whole ceremony lasts only a few minutes, but the seconds seem to drag out for eternity. I step forward and hold out my hand to West. He places the handle of my knife into my palm, and Genevieve fastens her bottom lip between her teeth, panic finally blossoming on her features. I take hold of her dress by the strap over her left shoulder and I quickly cut the material, slashing through it with ease. I do the same to the other side, and the white silk tumbles from her body, gathering in a pool at her feet. As I demanded of her, she's not wearing any underwear. She stands with her hands at her sides, fingers twitching reflexively, as if she wants to cover herself. I give her a look that lets her know just how displeased I will be with her if she does this, and something happens: a flash of anger lights up her face. Instead of hiding her embarrassment, Genevieve rolls her shoulders back and lifts her chin, staring me down. Fucking adorable. She thinks she can stand up to me? She thinks she's brave enough for what's to come? She has no idea how absolutely messed up and confusing her world is about to get. I'm going to have the time of my fucking life showing her. There will come a time, soon, when she will have to choose between me and her brothers, and she will not be able turn her back on me. She will beg for their deaths just so long as I continue to allow her into my bed. She'll turn her back on her blood in order to remain in my good graces. She won't just give me her heart. She'll give me her soul and everything else she holds dear, and I will take it all from her with a savage fucking smile on my face.

I begin to unbutton my shirt. "I hope you're ready. You understand what I require of you?"

She breathes out heavily, then nods. "You tell

me what you want, and I obey."

West bites down on his bottom lip, groaning under his breath. Vaughn remains silent, but I can see the anticipation glittering in his eyes. Genevieve shifts, clearly uncomfortable that my brothers appear to be growing excited. "Are they… are they going to…?"

"They're witnesses. They have to witness *everything*. That a problem?" This is how it used to be done back when Kings and Queens used to get married. A room full of people would stay and watch the newly weds fuck, just to make sure the marriage was consummated. The Bastien family have also adhered to this tradition for as long as anyone can remember. My mother and father, my grandparents, my great grandparents, on and on, forever. Genevieve's obviously repelled by the idea of so many people hanging around to watch us in bed. She frowns, deep lines marking her brow.

"It's not a problem," she whispers. "Let's just get it over with."

She assumes I'm going to screw her until I come and that will be that. She's sorely mistaken. Tonight won't be over until I've made *her* come. She needs to surrender to me in every way, and that includes her pleasure.

I strip down until I'm naked. Father Gustavo clears his throat, scratching at the back of his hand and his forearm like a junky craving his next fix. "I think, then, if that's all, I should be going—"

"You're not going anywhere," I snap. "If he tries to leave, cut his fucking balls off."

"Gladly," West says.

Gustavo opens his mouth, shocked, but then clearly thinks better of objecting and closes it again. Vaughn laughs very quietly under his breath, and Genevieve jumps at the unexpected sound of amusement.

"On the bed," I demand. She walks backwards until she reaches the bed, and then climbs up as I've instructed. She makes herself small, hugging her knees to her chest, watching me as I approach like a frightened deer.

"From here on out, there are no safe words," I tell her. "There's no backing out. You're here for me to use. You're here for me to do whatever the hell we want to you. You're here for me to own you. Nothing is off limits. Your body is my playground…and I like to play hard." I don't finish up this statement by asking her if this is okay. If it's not okay, then it's simply tough luck. She said the words. She relinquished control of her body and her life just now when she said 'I do.' She sold her soul to the devil, and now he's come to collect.

I climb up onto the bed and I push her roughly back onto the mattress. She stretches out long, but her arms and legs are rigid; I'm sure every part of her is screaming right now, begging her to fight me off, to get up and run, but she must know how futile that would be. If I wasn't already painfully fucking hard, the sight of her laid out like this would have my dick throbbing in less than cool second. She's incredible. Her breasts aren't huge, maybe a little more than a handful, but they're fucking amazing. Her nipples—small, a fragile shade of pink—are peaked and *so* ready for me to take into my mouth. The curve of her hips; the long, lean muscles in her legs; the slope of her collarbone, and the pool of her ink black hair around her head, arranged like a dark halo… every small piece of her on its own is flawless, but combined together she looks like a painting, a work of art that could never be replicated.

She sucks in a deep breath as I lean down, lowering my face toward hers. "I'm going to unlock your secrets," I growl, deep and low. "I'm going to discover every last one of them. Your body will betray you, and you'll hate me for it. You're going to want me, and you're going to be ashamed of the fact. There's no point trying to hide from the inevitable, though. There's no point trying to deny me. You're no longer Genevieve Kendrick. You're Genevieve Bastien. Get used to the name. The whole of New Orleans will know it soon…"

Callie Hart is the *USA Today* bestselling author of the Blood & Roses Series, the Chaos and Ruin series, and the Dead Man's Ink series. There are few real saints and sinners in her books; more often, the denizens of her stories are all very human. Broken, flawed, and always with the potential for redemption.

The first part of the New Orleans Nights series, Road to Ruin, will be released in 2017.

Shari Slade has put her devastatingly dark talents to use in the next story. Click to turn the page - if your heart is up to it…

BY SHARI SLADE

For the broken dolls, the lost boys, and the honeybadgers on a dark path home.

MICAH

TRASH PICKUP 4112

The message blinks on the screen, and I curse. Client 4112 is entirely too busy to retain my services. I'm an assassin. An executioner. Not a body disposal service for serial killers. This is the third slave he's broken in less than a year. I'm not one to judge anyone's dark proclivities, but this is sloppy.

I grab my gear.

Usually, 4112 is gone when I arrive for a pickup. But tonight, there's a light in the front window.

I approach with caution and let myself in the back door as I've done twice before.

"You'll have to finish her off for me. I've lost my appetite. She's in there." He points to the little soundproof room off the kitchen and smiles at me like he's doing me a favor. This sick fuck thinks I'm like him.

Maybe I am.

I've spent most of my life watching people from the shadows. Not because I'm some monster. Well, I am a monster. Just not of the physical variety. The people I watch are targets I've been hired to terminate. Mobster's rivals. Informants. Unfortunate witnesses in the wrong place at the wrong time. Loose ends. All of them the same to me—prey. And I'm the bullet that slams into their hearts.

I push the door open, and something rustles in the corner. My target. Her.

At first, she's nothing more than a jumble of sharp angles. Elbows and knees, bruised flesh. Blood. Then she shifts again, and my whole world tilts, like a kaleidoscope coming into focus. She's an angel. Still innocent despite the filth of this place. It shines from her—lights her up from within. Whatever 4112 did to her, he couldn't put it out.

My light has long since darkened—if I ever had

one—but hers could keep me warm.

Hair like spun copper riots in damp tangles around her face. Eyes like dark steel cloud with pain.

I watch her chest rise and fall with measured breaths. She squeezes her small hands into fists, and I recognize exactly what she's doing. In this horrible place, nearly beaten to death, with a hit man looming over her, with every reason to just let go…she's fighting for consciousness.

"Please." Her voice is scratchy and barely above a whisper, but that's all it takes. One word. One look at her bruised rosebud mouth and I'm done. Wrecked. I know deep in whatever's left of my soul—she's mine.

"I'll take her." I bark the statement back to 4112. Surprising myself as much as I surprise him.

"I'm afraid I don't understand."

My jaw clenches and I turn to face him. I hate when people play stupid, so it's a struggle not to throttle him. "Then I'll make it simple for you. You want her off your hands. I will take her. Go get her contract."

The light shifts in his eyes, cold and calculating. "Of course. We'll just negotiate terms."

"No," I snarl, then force myself to moderate my

tone. "You were going to pay me to kill her."

"I have the right to use her body as I see fit. You do not. Until we negotiate and settle on a price."

"She's broken. Damaged property. How much can she be worth?"

"I don't know. You're the one who wants her." 4112 smirks. "A very favorable bargaining position for me."

My arms tense. The urge to jam my gun into the soft flesh under his chin and ask him how favorable that position feels nearly overpowers me. But I force myself to relax. If I suddenly start killing my clients, it won't be good for business. "How much did you pay?"

"Fifty thousand. But I've trained her. She's worth more now. This pliant, come-hungry slut before you is my masterpiece."

I turn back to her and absorb even more of the horror. The dirty mat, the way her wrist is bent at an awkward angle. "She's a mess."

"That's the beauty, my friend." He brushes past me to crouch down on the floor beside her and smooth a hand over her thigh. Like petting the flank of a horse. "I bought her to break her. She signed up for this."

She flinches at his touch. A barely perceptible

movement, but I've spent my life watching with senses finely attuned. She may have signed up to be used. But she didn't sign up for his sick game. She didn't sign up for death. Did she?

Something unfamiliar flickers in my gut. I don't have a word for it. A terrible tenderness. A burn to possess her. To heal her and hurt her…just the way she needs.

My cock twitches. I would be a better owner. I would deliver her from this.

For what? The only thing I know how to deliver is death…bullets don't fall in love with their targets.

"Do you want to be mine?" I ask her. But she just stares blankly.

4112 snaps his fingers in front of her face. "Answer him. It's fine. I'm done punishing you."

"Please."

There's that word again. Such a pretty word on her lips. Not a word I hear very often. Mine is not a world of persuasion. My targets don't beg for their lives. They never have that chance. They're dead—a shot to the head, the heart—before they even know they're in my cross hairs.

I do some mental math. Client 4112 has already transferred ten thousand dollars into my numbered account. A nonrefundable deposit. Half of my cleaner fee. Balance due upon completion.

He'd have owed more for a hit, and he knows it.

I don't want to pay this man a penny, even as I know I would pay anything to keep this beautiful, broken doll. "I'll return your $10K. That's it."

"And I want a future job. A credit. A favor. Anything I want."

"Don't call me to clean up another slave."

He looks at the girl again, face softening. "I can't promise."

"If you call me for that, you won't like the way I choose to neutralize the problem."

"Have you ever owned a person? Held their very life in your hands? What am I saying? Of course, you've held lives in your hands. But this is different. Taking a person to the very edge of their humanity, seeing how far they'll bend before they break… It's heady." His eyes are bright. Fevered. "I've made myself a god. You will too. You'll see."

Bile rises in the back of my throat. "I could just kill you now and take her."

"You could. My associates would not like that at all. You're a businessman. Let's do business. I agree to your terms. If I have need of a…cleaner…I'll call another agent. Otherwise, you owe me a favor."

He extends his hand, but I don't want to touch him. I know owing this man anything is a mistake. The girl shifts again; her tiny whimpers of pain are a terrible sweetness. Her will to live… I recognize it for what it is. A fatal flaw. We're made of the same stuff, she and I. This broken girl's strength will be her destruction. Or mine.

It might be a mistake, but I have to have her. I nod my agreement, and our bargain is struck.

GIRL

Sir looms over me. "I'm going to transfer your ownership to this man. You know what that means? Answer yes or no."

He grabs my face, rough fingers dig into my cheeks, and the new man grunts his displeasure. "No touching."

Sir lets go, and my body relaxes. This new man is stronger than Sir. But that doesn't make sense. Nobody is stronger. Sir is the whole universe. Sir is letting go because he wants to let go. Not because the new man told him. That's the only way that makes sense.

"Answer," Sir commands.

"Yes." I know it means he can take me back at any point. He's told me so many times. He owns me forever. He can give me to whomever he wants, but I'll always be his.

"Take her." I flinch at the words. What have I done to displease Sir? To make him abandon me? I did everything he asked. Even when I thought it might kill me.

The new man gathers me in his arms. Everything hurts, but I don't have the energy to be afraid. This is what Sir wants, so it is good. I have to trust and accept.

MICAH

I don't have a place for her in my basement apartment. She deserves a fluffy bed with a mountain of pillows after what she's been through. All I have is darkness, four walls, and a cot. Everything is hard. Spartan. I grew up with even less; I see no need for pointless luxuries now.

Survival matters more than anything. She needs fluids and sleep. I set her on my cot and wrap her in a rough blanket.

"I'm Micah. What's your name?"

Her eyes are wide. "Whatever you want it to be."

"I know." This is the life she chose. One of servitude and pain. I can give her what she desires. "I've asked you a question, and you will answer it. You had a name once. Tell me now."

Tears well up in her eyes. "I'm sorry. I don't remember."

"We'll work on that, angel."

Panic flickers across her face, and she pulls the rough blanket tight around her. "Please don't call me angel. It's wrong."

A gruff laugh catches in my throat. What is wrong? A monster calling his new slave angel? A man making himself a god? A broken doll who can't see her own shine? "That's not how this works. You don't decide things. That's my job. I'm going to take care of you now. I'm going to give you everything you need."

"You're going to hurt me."

There's a sadness in her voice, a vulnerability that strips me to the quick, and I know she means something more by that than the twisted sex we both crave. *Smart girl.* "Of course I am. What shall

I call you while I do it? What name do you want on my lips while I destroy you?"

I don't tell her that I think I'm going to destroy us both.

She shakes her head, sandy lashes brushing her cheeks. "Sir called me slut. Whore."

"Those words mean nothing. They may tell me *what* you are, but they don't tell me who. Who are you here?" I touch the tip of my finger to her chest. "Inside. I own all of you now. Not just your body."

Her eyes squeeze shut, but she doesn't turn away. "Nothing. Nobody."

If I were a decent man, I'd drop her at a shelter. Or an emergency room. Somewhere with people who could actually help her while she can still be helped. Instead, I head to the cupboards over the sink in my efficiency kitchenette. Next to the first aid kit, I find a loose packet of hot cocoa mix. It had to be left behind by the previous tenant because there's no way I'd purchase that for myself. On impulse, I rip it open, drop the powder into a clean mug, and fill it with hot water from the tap. As I stir it, I watch the tiny pellet marshmallows reconstitute and disappear.

Her wrist is too weak to support the weight of the cup, so I press it to her lips. "Drink."

Tears roll down her cheeks as soon as the liquid hits her mouth. She gulps the watery sweetness, and some of it dribbles down her face. I set the mug on the floor beside the bed, open the battered first aid kit, and begin to tend to her wounds.

Her tongue darts out, swiping across her chin, catching the drops she'd failed to swallow. Whatever husk of a heart I have nearly breaks for the untamed sweetness of it.

"Thankyouthankyou." Her gratitude is too much, too effusive for nothing more than tepid water and sugar. It's sad. Deeply sad. I wonder what her life was like before she started this one. I think maybe she was always this sad, but I'm desperate to know.

"I'm going to call you *dolorita*," I tell her as I wind a brown bandage around her delicate arm. "Do you know what that means?"

"No," she says, still licking her lips, obviously savoring every molecule of chocolate. That she can enjoy anything—want anything—after her time with 4112 is unbelievable. I wonder what she'll enjoy after her time with me.

I take a sip from the cup myself—maybe I've stumbled on to some magic elixir—and nearly gag. I haven't had anything but water or black coffee for decades, and this is like drinking syrup. I must have had cocoa as a child, at school or in one of the group homes, but I don't remember this taste at all. It doesn't matter. There's never been much room in my life for sweetness. But her gratitude? I could become accustomed to having that.

I dry her mouth with the edge of the blanket. "*Dolorita* means little sorrow. It suits you."

DOLORITA

For what seems like weeks, he does very little but leave me food and water. No more warm cocoa, but I'm a little relieved. Those few sips were delicious but they gave me a terrible bellyache. Each night, he watches me undress and stands outside the shower stall while I wash myself under the steaming jets. His hazel eyes rake over my naked body—a steady, searching gaze. Hard. Clinical. He does not touch me.

I don't understand. I exist to be touched. To be used. Each night, I expect Sir to return for me. At first with anticipation, but later with growing fear.

Micah tells me I'm his now.

The plain white bar of soap on the shelf smells just like him. I rub it over my body and imagine him sliding it over his bronze muscles, scrubbing his close-cropped hair, soaping his penis with the harsh lather. I slip my soapy hands over my breasts and imagine his hands on me. Rough fingers, thick and invasive. I dip between my legs and furtively brush over my clit.

He clucks his displeasure, and I shiver. That subtle reprimand is a balm to my soul. I'm not to touch myself. He will give me what I need when he decides I need it.

Outside the shower, I dry off with the same white towel I used the day before. It's a little stiff, but it's not dirty. He watches me do this too.

There are no other toiletries besides a tube of generic baking powder toothpaste. Even so, it feels like a trip to a spa after my time with Sir. I haven't been clean since… I can't remember. Now I fall asleep each night with damp hair and brushed teeth. Safe and warm on my cot.

For the first time in a long time, I try to focus on the past. It's slippery and sharp. Remembering feels dangerous. The girl I see in flashes of memory can't be me.

When I finish my nightly routine to his

satisfaction, he hands me a clean white undershirt from his dresser drawer. The soft cotton hangs loose over my thin frame and lands just below my bottom, barely concealing anything, making me more aware of my nakedness than actual nudity. On him, these shirts stretch taut over his biceps and pecs and tuck into dark work pants.

"Your bruises are healed?"

It's the first question he's asked me since the night he took me home. I tug at the hem of the shirt and nod. The last had turned yellow and faded away sometime over the past few days.

"Speak, *dolorita*. Do you hurt anywhere?"

I do. My old injuries are gone, but I have a new ache. I remember his cluck as I showered. My heart hammers, but I can't resist. I have nothing to lose. Dropping the shirt, I let my fingers drift between my thighs again to cup my pussy. "Here."

His lips part and slip into a terrifying smile. "Good. From this day forward, the only marks on your creamy flesh will be mine."

"Will you mark me now?" I ask before I can stop myself. Speaking without permission is a grave offense. Sir would backhand me into the mirror without hesitation, and I'd deserve it. Micah only raises an eyebrow.

He grabs me by the hips and pushes me up onto the small counter in the bathroom. My legs are spread, but he pushes my knees farther apart. "Wider. I want to see all of you first."

I scoot forward like I'm on an exam table and spread my legs as wide as I can. Cool air plays over my damp folds, and shame heats my cheeks. It's an unfamiliar feeling. Sir's unrelenting cruelty stripped me of all my embarrassments. I wonder what else Micah will give back to me. And if I'll be allowed to keep it.

He kneels between my legs, flattens his palms against my inner thighs, and brings his face close enough that I can feel his breath fan across my sex. "This is mine, *dolorita*. You don't touch it unless I tell you to touch it. Do you understand?"

Each word whispers over me and sends shivers of pleasure straight up to my nipples. His fingers dig into my thighs even harder to stop my squirming.

"Yes."

"Now pinch your clit for me."

I slip my hand between us and find the throbbing bundle of nerves with my thumb and forefinger. It feels so good to put a little pressure there, to squeeze and release, squeeze and release. A little friction and I'd be—

And then the pleasure is too sharp, his hand is over mine, forcing me to squeeze even harder until it isn't pleasure at all. Until it's something hot and terrible.

"Don't stop pinching," he commands, like I'd give this up if given a choice.

I nod. Then he's standing, his thick cock jutting out from his open pants.

"I can't decide if I want you to suck me or fuck me, so we'll do both."

He traces the curve of my lip with the tip of his finger and then forces three of them into my mouth. They're thick and salty, not so different from a penis, but they curve a little toward the back of my throat. When I gag, he makes approving noises and rocks them back and forth. Harder and harder. Forcing me backward on the counter until my head hits the wall. I keep sucking, swirling my tongue around the invasion, retching a little each time he goes deep.

He shoves inside my pussy with a single thrust. I'm not ready for him. His thickness stretches me to the point of pain, and I can barely take all of him. I feel too full. Even the slightest movement is like being torn. Still, my clit throbs between my pinching fingers, a white-hot ball of need.

"I'm going to come all over you tonight," he grunts between rough thrusts. "You're going to sleep with my jizz dripping down your thighs and smeared on your face. I might even come on you while you're sleeping. You're going to wake up crusted with my seed, the smell of me so strong in your nostrils you'll never smell anything else. Now that you're clean, I'm going to make you filthy again."

We fall into a beautiful rhythm of degradation and pain for days and days.

MICAH

Every inch of her body is mine. Every orifice. Every thought that plays across her unguarded face. It's everything I never knew I wanted, and still, I want more.

I hate it. Wanting.

I punish her for making me want things I've never had before. Companionship. Conversation. Comfort.

I've already bent my rules too much. No property, no public, no details…

Property is weakness. Anything you own is just something for your enemies to steal. The thought of anyone taking my *dolorita* slashes through me like a jagged knife.

But I want to take her out into the world. I want to slip a frilly dress over her naked body and sit beside her at a restaurant while we eat a beautiful meal. I want to shove my fingers into her pussy under the table while she politely tells the waiter our order. The dress is folded neatly in the bottom drawer, just waiting for me to cave further.

I want to know who she was before. I want her name. I want to investigate her past. I've already hired someone to make the discreet inquiries.

I let her call me by my name simply because I want to wrench it from her throat as her pussy muscles rippled around my cock.

I might as well carry a blinking neon sign over my head. Compromised. Vulnerable. Target.

I bought a fucking box of hot cocoa. She's done this to me.

I keep her mouth full of my cock as much as possible. It's much safer than letting her talk.

DOLORITA

I wake, disoriented and starving for air.

My lips stretch over a thick invasion, drool pools at the corners of my mouth, the acrid scent of warm skin fills my flaring nostrils. My screams are muffled at the back of my throat, but his voice is a rough half whisper tearing through the darkness. "Don't you dare bite down. You know what happens."

I squirm at the reminder, my nipples still sore, the bruises over my breasts still fresh. I force myself to be still, to relax my jaw and accept the force of his bucking hips.

He spurts, and I swallow it down quickly, making the greedy noises I already know he likes. This is a gift he is giving me—I know that now—and I will accept it with whatever silent thanks I can offer.

He saved me.

He brushes a hand over my cheek as he slips free, a few seconds of fingertips skimming the hollow created by his exiting cock, the briefest contact—if it weren't for the times before, I'd think it accidental. The tenderness makes me shiver.

"Spread your legs."

I do, and he touches me between them. Tests me. Where his touch had been nearly tender before, now it's clinical. "You are not wet."

I shake my head, shame heating my cheeks. Dryness. Wetness. I've been chided for both. Either. It's not the secretions of my body that are embarrassing. It's the way my body won't do what makes him happy on command.

"I thought I bought a come-hungry slut. Was that a lie?"

I shake my head again.

"Use your words. Tell me what you are."

"Come-hungry." My voice cracks with disuse, and the filthy words do their job, warming my cheeks, starting a steady throb in my clit.

"Come-hungry what?" he urges, rolling my nipple between his thumb and forefinger. Twisting to the point of pain.

"Come-hungry slut," I pant, nearly spitting the last word, hating it and loving it at the same time, hating the way it burns me up from the inside and loosens my body.

I hear the crack of his palm before I feel the sting. Tingling heat spreads across my face. "Don't make me regret letting you speak. Say it right."

I stare at the ceiling, tears pricking my eyes,

and imagine my other life. Before. The one where I had a name. The one where I wore sensible slacks and went to work at the fellowship hall and never said words like the ones he wants me to say.

He brings it back to me with every bit of kindness. With every tender mercy he shows me. The longer he keeps me from the one who made me forget. Sir. I don't want to go back to him.

"I'm your come-hungry slut," I sob, fear and relief mingling as he releases my nipples.

"That's right." He strokes me between my legs again. Pets me. "That's exactly what you are. Nothing more. I should fuck you dry to punish you for forgetting, but I have plans for you later today and I don't want to bring you too damaged.

I jerk to squeeze my legs shut, but he's faster than I am, flattening his palms over my thighs and pinning me down. "Ah, ah, ah. It's not him coming. I've told you. You're mine now. He's never taking you back."

I know, but my body still acts on reflex. I can't help it. My heart beats a wild tattoo in my chest, and I can hardly think. Not him, not him, not him. My mind races, and it's only fingernails digging into my hips that bring me back to the present.

"Shh, shh. Should I have you touch yourself

until you're ready for me? Would that get your head back where it belongs?"

I nod. Too eagerly because his face darkens, lips turning up at the corners in a wicked smile. "Oh, no. That won't do at all. You'd bring yourself to orgasm, wouldn't you?"

"No, I wouldn't. I promise."

And then he's pinching my nipples again. "Did I tell you to speak? No, you can't be trusted to touch yourself at all. I'll have to do it myself. But how?"

He draws a finger down the curving underside of my breast and over my belly. My mind races, following the heat of his touch. He spreads my lips, letting air caress my most secret places. "Maybe I'll pinch your little clit again until you scream. If you're going to make noise, at least you can make the kinds of noises I'm interested in hearing."

He taps the small bundle of nerves, and it's like he struck a match, pleasure zinging like fire as I buck up off the cot. I don't make a sound.

"Maybe I'll lick you. I won't even touch your clit, just spread my saliva around until you're wet enough for what I want. Use your words now. Tell me you want me to lick your pussy. Beg me pretty, and maybe I'll let you come sometime today." Oh God, I want that and I don't. If he puts his mouth on me, I'll come for sure, no matter the consequences. He slaps my mound, stoking the white-hot center and sending pleasure radiating through me again.

"Please. Please. Lick my pussy. Put your tongue on my cunt. Please." Every word is like a tiny slap. These are his words, but they've become mine. Everything of mine is his. His. Mine. My thoughts go hazy as his breath fans hot over my slit, his tongue dipping into my folds.

One lazy flick and he pulls back. "Your cream is all over my tongue now. Was it the begging that did it or the dirty talk? Never mind, we'll figure that out later. We've got all the time in the world."

I can barely form a coherent thought as he slicks his tongue over me again. Barely remember my name. But I remember the one from before. His shadow hangs heavy over me no matter what this one says. He'll be back.

"This is very generous of me. Say thank you while I lick you. Keep saying it."

I repeat it like the litany he wants. One long word. A string of syllables to drown out anything. Everything. "Thankyouthankyouthankyou."

The orgasm builds and builds and builds, doubling over on itself until I feel infinite. Until

I feel like I'll die if I come or die if I don't. His tongue slides around my clit, swoops down to gather more of my juices. My cream. And then spreads it around. Never going where I need it. Never touching the sharpness of my desire. Thankyouthankyouthankyou.

Then he pulls back, and the wave of heat races away from the shore in a shuddering riptide of loss. I am wet and writhing. Lips still swollen from the invasion of his cock. Empty. Bereft.

I bite back the please threatening to tumble from my mouth. I can learn.

"Good girl," he says, stroking my cheek again. "Now turn over. I don't want to see your face while I fuck you."

MICAH

Her teeth sink into her bottom lip, and I relish her disappointment. Almost giving her what she wants and taking it away is my favorite torment.

There is no torture like hope.

She rolls over and gets herself up on her knees and elbows. Presenting her ass to me like an animal in heat. I spank her because I can. That's all she is—an animal, an object—I tell myself over and over. My palm smacks against her flesh in a steady rhythm. Until my hand is numb and her ass cheeks are rosy red. Until I believe the lies I tell myself.

"Please, Micah."

Her desperate whimpers break my conviction. The way she says my name. Insolent and innocent. *Fuck*. I want to plunge into the slick heat of her cunt and fill her with my come. Mark her inside too. Put a fucking baby in her.

The thought twists in my gut. A monster's child. It's too much.

Bent over her, lips close to her ear, I grab a fistful of her hair and shove my other hand under her mouth.

"I'm going to take your asshole. Spit in my hand. Do a good job or don't. It's the only lube you get. One, two, three—" Tears hit my palm first, then something more viscous. "Nine, ten."

My palm is shiny, but it's not much. This will hurt her, but she made that choice. Maybe I didn't give her very long to…produce…but I did give her the opportunity.

I slick her fluids over my cock and press the tip to the tight entrance. "Resist me, *dolorita*. Fight against my cock. Help me wreck you. I thought I wanted you whole for our meeting, but I don't. I want you unable to sit or move or breathe without thinking of me invading your body."

Her muscles tense beneath me. "Wha—"

She starts to ask a question, but it's swallowed up in a scream as I push deeper into her channel. "We're going to meet a man, *dolorita*. A man who acquires women. He says they ask to be sold. Did you answer a filthy ad?"

"Noooo."

"Did you go looking for something nasty on the internet and find something worse than you'd ever dared dream?"

"No-no-no."

I push deeper and reach around to thrum her clit until her legs are quaking. "It's okay, angel. I know you did. He's going to look at you, and I'm going to make him tell us what he knows. I'm going to give you back your past. Whether you want it or not."

If you enjoyed Little Sorrow and want to read more of Micah and his *dolorita*, Shari will be releasing more of their story soon!

If you'd like to read another dark, dirty-talking man right now, check out Noah, the dangerous enforcer of The Devil's Host MC.

When a big scary biker shows up at Jimmy's Diner fifteen minutes before the end of my shift—covered in tattoos and looking at me like I'm on the menu—I should flip the open sign to closed.

But I don't.

I'm too used to doing what I've been told. Too used to working and struggling and surviving to do anything different. A closed sign wouldn't stop him anyway. He's here to collect a debt. And I'm the only one left to pay.

T.M. Frazier has packed the next story with hot-as-hell bikers you may have met in the KING series... but you've never seen them like this before. We suggest you GET READING!

His Possession

BY T.M. FRAZIER

KING

White smoke snaked into the night sky from under the closed lid of the huge-ass grill taking up half the back wall against the garage. The smell of sweet smoky barbecue permeated the yard. My mouth watered and my stomach growled just thinking about the piles of ribs Billy was cooking to perfection underneath that lid. The stars were out in full force. The moon was full overhead, covering the bay in a bright yellow blanket of light. The air was wet and hot. The music deafening.

I fucking loved it.

Our three kids, along with Trey and Bo were

with Dre's dad and his new girlfriend at some swanky hotel over The Causeway. I imagined Max and Sammy running up and down the hallways, knocking over room service trays and drawing all over the walls in crayon. I laughed at the thought.

The music changed from an old Bush song to something by Miranda Lambert. I glanced over and spotted Ray bent over at the waist, screwing with the settings on the radio. Her perfect ass swayed to the beat. Her butt cheeks peeked out the bottom of her cut-offs, which made my palm twitch with the need to mark my girl's perfect pale skin. Just a little smack would do the trick. Something others could see when she bent over.

Something to remind everyone that she was MINE.

I looked around the yard and found Billy enjoying the same view I was. I gave him a warning glare, a growl rumbled deep within my throat. His eyes widened and he looked to the sky, whistling to himself.

Damn fucking right.

The song changed again. This time to something poppy and auto-tuned that made me cringe. But not Ray. She was smiling and dancing to the beat. Ray liked to play the role of amateur DJ when we had a party, the problem was that she never let a song play all the way to the end, always changing it before it barely reached the chorus, which made me laugh and made the crowd stop and groan.

As if she felt my eyes on her Ray looked back at me. The fire from the pit behind her crackled and popped, making her icy blue eyes look even brighter. When she winked at me I swear to fucking God that if Bear and Thia hadn't walked up at that moment I would have stormed across the yard, pushed her shorts and panties to the side, and fucked her up against the speaker. Crowd be damned.

Fuck, at least then maybe she'd let an entire song play.

"You gonna snort all that shit at once?" Bear asked, pointing with his cigarette to the pile of blow I was emptying from a little baggie into the palm of my hand. He smiled. "I mean, it's a party and all and I know it's been a bit since we've had one without the kids, but you planning on being awake until next fucking Thursday or something?"

"Not exactly," I replied. Bear smirked and wrapped his arm around Thia's shoulder. She looked up at him and smiled, but there was worry in her eyes. He kissed her on the top of the head and chuckled. "He's like six minutes away, and he's in good hands, Ti."

Thia sighed. "I know," she said. "I'm fine." Her stiff posture, along with the way she was chomping on the corner of her thumbnail, gave away that she was anything but fine.

"Why don't you go inside and call to check up. I want my girl to be able to enjoy herself instead of worrying all night long. Besides, I gotta see why the fuck King here has a fist full of blow," Bear said to Thia.

She smiled and gave him a quick peck on the lips. "I'll be right back," she said, but before she could turn to leave, Bear pulled her in and held both sides of her face.

"You forgot something," he growled, pressing his lips to hers, kissing her hard and deep. She stood on her tiptoes and wrapped her arms around his neck.

I cleared my throat. When Bear finally released her, Thia's cheeks were bright red and her eyes half-lidded with lust. She stumbled a little and Bear gave her a knowing smile. "Where was I going again?" she asked breathlessly.

Bear reached behind her into her back pocket and pulled out her phone. He handed it to her.

"You gonna call and check on Trey, beautiful." He turned her around by the shoulders and smacked her on the ass. She flashed him an embarrassed smile and took off without another word, her phone already to her ear and a smile on her face by the time she reached the top step of the porch.

"Follow me," I said to Bear. He put out his cigarette on the bottom of his boot and followed me across the yard.

I tapped Preppy on the shoulder. When he turned around I threw a cloud of blow directly into his face. Bear howled out a laugh from beside me. In true Preppy fashion, he inhaled deeply through his nose. I laughed at my best friend, because it was fucking impossible not to laugh when he was around.

And thank fucking GOD he's around.

"Shit's expensive, boss-man," Preppy said, wiping the excess powder from under his eye, rubbing it on his gums. "Things really did change while I was gone. Didn't think you were one to waste this shit." He smiled and his pupils grew ten times their normal size.

"Rules don't apply today, you should know that," Bear said to Preppy, fishing a joint out from the inner pocket of his cut.

Preppy laughed and took a swig from the whiskey bottle he was holding.

"You have no fucking clue what day it is, do you?" I asked.

Preppy shrugged. "Thursday?"

"It's your fucking birthday, asshole," Bear pointed out, playfully shoving Preppy who staggered sideways.

Preppy crinkled his forehead. "It's my…birthday?" he asked, like he couldn't believe it.

"It's your birthday," I repeated.

"Wow. I haven't really been thinking about it." Preppy grinned and took another swig. "Man, I can't believe I'm twenty-fucking-nine. That's fucking crazy to me. I'm almost as old as you two over-the-hill motherfuckers."

"Prep," Bear said, "you're not twenty-nine today."

"You're thirty," I added.

Preppy took a step back and for a second looked like he was doing math. Then he started silently counting something off on his fingers. "No…fuck. I missed a birthday? I mean, it makes sense, but I didn't really think about it. Fuck. I'm… thirty? Holy shit. I'm an old fucking man and I didn't even know it."

"You're not old. You're still younger than us."

"But I haven't prepared to be thirty," Preppy said, staring down into the whiskey bottle.

"I'm pretty sure there isn't any preparation involved," Bear said.

"Sure there is," Preppy argued. "My pants for example. They're too low. I need to buy ones with higher waists. I don't even suck loudly on my teeth after a meal."

I rolled my eyes and grabbed a beer from the cooler.

Preppy continued. "I mean, I don't even know what time Jeopardy starts and I've never been a morning person but I suppose I could learn to wake up at four a.m. to start my day of sitting on the porch. Dinner time at three p.m. Shit, there's a lot to consider here." He sat in the grass and Bear knelt down to comfort him.

That's when I noticed that Ray was no longer at the speaker and the light was on in the tattoo studio window. The possessive need I always felt for her took over and by the time I realized I was moving, I'd left my friends behind and was already halfway across the yard on my way to the garage.

To my girl.

MINE.

RAY

The studio was dark except for the small lamp on the side table. The party was raging just outside the window. I looked down to the paper on the desk and smiled.

"Are you hiding from me, Pup?" King boomed from the doorway, startling me from my thoughts.

I gasped and spun around, dropping the pencil in my hand. "You scared the shit out of me," I said.

King's biceps rippled as he grabbed the header of the doorframe, leaning forward into the room his abs flexed under his tight black t-shirt. His dark jeans were slung low on his hips. His emerald green eyes were glowing with desire. His eyes looked me over, licking me from head to toe and back again.

I knew that look.

I fucking loved that look.

My nipples hardened and my mouth fell open. My lips parted. My thighs shook with need.

King took a step into the room and I backed up, almost tripping over my fallen pencil.

"I thought I didn't scare you anymore?" King asked slowly with a chuckle from deep in his throat. He raised an eyebrow, the one with the small white scar that ran through it. His words were dark and seductive, dripping from his full lips as he approached.

"You…you don't," I stuttered. I turned and bent over to pick the pencil up off the floor. His thighs brushed the back of mine and when I stood up his hard body was behind me. His hands on my shoulders. He brushed the hair from my neck and I shuddered. The warmth of his body sent tingles of awareness over my skin which prickled with anticipation.

"Don't lie to me, Pup," he said, trailing his hands down the sides of my arms and back up my torso, stopping to brush the underside of my breasts. My knees buckled but he held me up and pressed me harder against him. His impossibly large cock prodded my backside through his jeans and I moaned at the sensation. "Why are you in here?"

"I had an idea for a sketch," I said breathlessly. "I wanted to get the bones of it down while it was still in my head."

"What was it?" King asked, flexing his hips against my backside. He growled in my ear and I arched my back into him. He pulled my arms behind me and held my wrists together with one hand while the other trailed down my torso and popped the button of my shorts open. I shook my head.

"Tell me," King demanded, shoving his hand inside my shorts, his fingers playing with the edge of my panties, dipping inside only to pull them out again. I writhed my hips, needing more.

"No, Pup. You show me what I want to see and I'll give you what you want. I'll make you come harder than you've ever come before. I'll make you scream my fucking name so loud every single person outside will hear you over the music." He tightened his grip on my wrists and circled his thumb over my damp panties. He groaned. My nipples were impossibly hard. "I can feel how much you want me. I can fucking SMELL how much you want me to make you come. Show me, Pup and I'll make it all better for you." His words released a flush of wetness between my legs and if he kept it up my entire body would be a puddle on the floor.

"The desk," I said, my voice sounding harsh and desperate.

Without releasing me, King led me over to the desk. He bent down slightly in order to get a better view of the sketch I had just outlined. It was him, sitting on a bed in his room at the end of the hall. The light from the door shining on his face.

"The night we met," King said, almost like he couldn't believe it.

"Yes," I replied. "It was supposed to be a surprise."

"It's…it's fucking beautiful," King said. I was about to reply when he pushed me over to the couch and pressed my chest against the armrest. "Since you showed me what I wanted to see I'm going to give you what you need. But first, there is something else I want to see."

Before I could respond, my shorts and panties were around my ankles and King's nose was against my pussy. "Fucking beautiful," he said, taking a long inhale. I wiggled my hips, reaching for what I was seeking, but he grabbed my hips and held me still as he flattened his tongue and gave me a long slow lick from my clit to my ass. "You taste like fucking heaven."

The pressure in my lower stomach was building at an impossibly fast rate. Every single touch and lick set my nerve endings on fire. I was about to combust when he flipped me over, picking me up only to set me down with my back against the floor. He kneeled between my legs and unbuckled his jeans, releasing his massive cock which bobbed up and down between us. I licked my lips and a bead of moisture glistened from the top of the thick head. He fisted his shaft. "Why did you draw that?" he asked, his voice rough and scratchy.

"It was going to be a gift for you. For Valentine's Day." King pushed his index finger inside my pussy and I lifted my hips off the ground. He pulled it back out again.

"Keep going," King ordered, removing his finger from me. I groaned at the loss. He lifted his shirt over his head and tossed it to the side, revealing his beautiful body full of colorful tattoos.

"I…" I stammered as he again pushed a finger inside me. "I wanted you to see how I saw you that night. I wanted you to remember it always."

King's response was a groan. He crooked his finger slightly to reach the spot that had me pushing back against his hand. The pressure built and built. The walls of my pussy contracting around his finger until again he removed his hand.

A second later something much larger was prodding at my entrance. Hot thick heat pushing inside of me. He stopped when only the head of his cock was in and it pulsed. I cried out. Needing more.

"Thank you for making me look like a man and less like…" he paused. A criminal. A villain.

I reached up and touched the side of his face. He closed his eyes and leaned into my palm. "My Sweet Villaintine," I giggled. His eyes shot open and he surged inside of me, pushing himself in all the way to the hilt and I screamed in both pleasure and pain.

"I think we both know that I'm not sweet," King said, pulling out only to thrust back in even harder.

"No?" I asked, meeting his gaze. "Then prove it."

King started to pump into me furiously, each stroke igniting the desire I'd never stopped feeling for him into an inferno of need and want. It was about more than sex and orgasms. It was about pure animal desire. A true feeling of being with the person made just for you. About being owned and owning in return. He fucked me like he loved me. He fucked me like he hated me. He fucked me harder and harder. I lifted up against each of his thrusts, each one more powerful than the last until we were both screaming out our orgasms into the small room, our cries echoing off the walls and ceiling. I didn't just come. It was more like a powerful explosion of pleasure, pulsing from my pussy and extending to the rest of my body. King groaned long and loud when he finished, first inside of me before pulling out suddenly, jerking his shaft as he spread me open with his fingers, releasing long streams of wet warmth over my exposed pussy and clit.

King collapsed onto the floor next to me, immediately pulling me on top of his strong chest while we both recovered from the mind numbing pleasure. "Happy early Valentine's Day," I said with a chuckle.

He smiled into my hair. "Don't you mean Villaintine's Day?"

I laced my fingers through his, circling the wedding ring on his left hand with my thumb. I looked up into his deep green eyes and sighed deeply. "My sweet Villaintine."

T.M. Frazier is a *USA TODAY* BESTSELLING AUTHOR best known for her KING SERIES. She was born on Long Island, NY. When she was eight years old she moved with her mom, dad, and older sister to sunny Southwest Florida where she still lives today with her husband and daughter.

The excerpt above contained characters from T.M.'s bestselling KING series. Want to meet KING and his fucked-up, sexy-as-hell friends? Start the series with KING (and then continue with TYRANT, LAWLESS, SOULLESS and many more books)!

Lili St. Germain features her brand-new *California Blood* series over the page - can you handle the heat? Or maybe we should ask: **Can you handle the darkness?** *Guess you'd better find out...*

Enjoy the first iteration of Rome + Avery!

♡
Lili St.
Germain
x y x

BY LILI ST. GERMAIN

ROME

THERE IS A GIRL ON HER KNEES IN FRONT OF me. A beautiful girl. I don't know her name, or her age, or what she loves or who she aches for; but I know her better than anyone has ever known her. Better than her mother, who grew her from a tiny seed and birthed her and fed her and nurtured her. I know her better than her father, who held her newborn feather-weight body and loved her so fiercely, it probably caused him physical pain; the knowledge all fathers of girls are burdened with, that one day their baby daughters will grow up and become things for men to inflict their own anger upon.

I know her better than the family she grew up with, the people she knew, the people she adored.

I know her better than anyone, because I know her sorrow. I have kissed my cracked lips against her hurt. I have seen inside her soul, every time I hold it between my palms and squeeze until it bleeds, *and what a pretty soul it is.*

I know everything about her, but she knows nothing about me. She thinks I'm a madman, and that slams into me like a knife every time she raises those doe eyes to me and begs. I see the cogs in her brain turn as she tries to outsmart me, to outthink me, to outplay me.

But what move could a naked girl on her knees ever have? What weapon? What *thing* that could save her? That could save us both?

She has nothing of power in this place, and we both know it. Her only power is her obedience. Her silence. Her ability to endure.

She is slipping. She is *losing her mind.*

I don't dare tell her that I am losing mine, too. Because there are three things I know for sure. Firstly, that we will die in this room. I think she'll go before me, because I'll have to choke the life out of her with my own hands; but I won't be far behind her. My death will be far more horrible. I'll need to preserve her beauty in death, but my role in this story is not a beautiful one. I am the monster. I am her torturer. Whatever my final moments entail, there will be rivers of my blood as I cut into my own guilty flesh and try to dig out an eleventh-hour salvation.

The second thing I know is that I'm going to hurt her so much before this is over. Brutally. Sadistically. She knows it, too, her big eyes shining with unspilled tears and terror. There's still hope inside her—a hope so thick I could almost plunge my hand into her chest and pluck it from her ribcage, along with her heart.

The third thing I know is that *this is not my fault*. She thinks I'm crazy. Everybody will think I'm crazy. I am not a good man – I am a very, very bad man. I have lied, I have cheated, I have killed – I am a monster, but I am not *this* monster. I only hope that in her final moments, I might be able to tell her this. As I drain the life from her, I pray that I can send her off to sleep one last time with the knowledge that I only ever wanted to save her.

But I digress.

There is a girl on her knees in front of me. A beautiful girl. She whimpers as I squeeze her cheeks, as I force her mouth open and glimpse her wet, pink tongue. I don't know her name, or her age, or what she loves or who she aches for. I only know that in a moment, she will ache for me.

AVERY

The man I'm kneeling in front of looks pretty ordinary for a psychopath. I'm ashamed to admit that when I saw him across the bar at The Cleopatra Club in downtown San Francisco, I would have even called him handsome. Cheekbones that could cut glass and a gaze so intense a less confident girl would have looked away. I didn't look away. I was a stupid girl, and now I am being punished. I caught his eye across the bar and my cheeks flushed. Moisture pooled in my panties, a damp spot that he found later, in this place, with rough fingers and a desperate need to sate himself while my bound arms went numb underneath me and my tears pasted his cruel red blindfold to my eyelashes.

I do not think he is handsome right now. The word for the man looming above me, his jaw so tight his teeth might shatter inside his mouth, a long-stemmed red rose clenched in one fist? Definitely not handsome.

No, the word I would use to describe my captor is *terrifying*.

From his back pocket he pulls out a length of red fabric. More blindfold. Fresh. I bled too much over the last one. I flinch as he presses the new material to my eyes and knots it behind my head. He's turning my world red, one blindfolded torture session at a time.

"Stick your tongue out," he says. His voice is always quiet, barely a gravelly rasp. He sang to me the first night I was here; fractured nursery rhymes and Christmas songs, the only words he claimed to remember. His voice is beautiful. He was nice to me then. Nicer, at least. He begged me to forgive him in those first hours as he dragged a washcloth over my broken and battered body. And when he pressed my thighs apart and raped me for the first time, I couldn't see him crying, but I felt every single one of his tears fall upon my naked chest as I drifted in and out of consciousness. And then the singing. He held me to his chest and sang to me as I drifted back into the inky blackness.

That was before I woke up with the collar around my neck. Now, he doesn't hold me. He doesn't sing to me. He stays as far away as possible from me unless he is trying to break me with the pain.

I stick my tongue out, because I don't want to be punished. My entire body is on edge. I loathe the dark. I hate that I can't see, even though I know what happens next. Something warm and hard will enter my mouth, and he'll push into my throat until I gag. He'll do it until he comes down my throat, and only then will he let me pull away. Last time he was so rough I threw up, and he hasn't let me eat since. I have no measurement of time, but I've gone to sleep and woken up twice since then. I've been sticking my finger down my throat and practicing suppressing my gag reflex ever since.

So when something small and sharp presses into the centre of my tongue, I scream, bringing my hands up to knock the blindfold from my face. He's threatened to cut my tongue out before. Is this is? Is this what he's doing? God, please no.

A crack erupts at the base of my throat as electricity sears into my skin through two metal prongs. When I'm bad, he delivers a shock to me through the dog shock collar that he's locked on to my neck. I am bad a lot.

I get shocked so many times I've lost count. My captor specializes in cruelty.

I'm screaming, because it hurts, and because the vibration in my throat when I make a noise pushes the two metal prongs just a tiny bit further away from me. I don't know if the shock is any less intense, because sometimes it is so blinding hot and sharp-stinging that I lose consciousness.

"Put the blindfold back on!" he snaps, my nameless master. I hear what sounds like worry in his voice. Desperation. Does he not want me to see as he cuts my tongue out? I wait in suspension as the electricity passes through my body, my existence temporarily halted as I see bright white stars explode in my vision, the taste of metal thick and cloying on my tongue.

I am beginning to forget things, and I am sure the shocks are the reason why my mind is starting to betray me.

The shock finally passes, my fingertips itching and the hair on my head wild with the static left behind. I reach up with tentative fingers and start to replace the blindfold, pausing as I see the red rose still in his hand. The long stem is still dotted with thorns, and as the inside of my mouth begins to itch, I realize *this* is what broke the delicate tissue of my tongue open until blood pooled in my mouth.

"Are you going to cut my tongue out?" I whisper. My throat hurts from the sharp metal electrodes. My tongue hurts from the rose thorn. My head hurts from the knowledge that this could go on until I die.

He closes his eyes and takes a deep breath. Almost as if he's waiting. Then he opens his eyes again, fixes his cool gaze on me, and stares.

"No."

He doesn't normally answer my questions. Normally I'm screaming them instead of murmuring them. Emboldened, I decide to ask another, even if it ends up hurting me.

"Why'd you cut my tongue?" I ask. "Why the rose?"

He looks at the ceiling, a small noise coming from his throat as he unzips his jeans and holds his erection in his open palm.

"Lubrication," he says finally. Before I can really hear what he's said, my blindfold is knotted back in place over my eyes and I'm gagging on hot flesh again.

ROME

There are rules that the voice in my head gives me and rules I make up myself.

The voice has simple rules: *Do everything he says. Make her suffer. Never disobey.*

My rules are murkier: Be as merciful as possible. Make her suffering quick. Only hurt her as much as the collar would hurt her. It frightened me, the first time I saw its effects on her body. It can deliver small warning zaps, but on the first day, when she was having a meltdown and clawing at the walls, the collar must have been turned up to the maximum settings, because it shocked her so badly she lost control of her bladder and pissed all over herself. She had a seizure, too, just for a few seconds, convulsing on her back on the hard floor. The collar's since been turned down. She hasn't lost control again when the sharp crack sounds at her neck, but she still screams every time.

I try as much as I can to limit her suffering. I know she hates me, and I don't blame her – I hate myself more. If the voice tells me to rape her, I do it as quickly as possible. If I have to do something that would kill her, I let her be shocked instead.

Right now, I'm rutting my dick into her throat. The blood from her tongue does indeed provide a nice lubricant, but I'm not getting any enjoyment out of this. No, I'm repulsed. The only reason I can get hard in the first place is because the voice makes me take these pills that make my dick rock-hard for hours at a time.

Tell her to open her mouth, the voice says. *Fuck her throat until she can't breathe. Show her she is nothing.* The doe-eyed girl can't hear the voice. Only I can hear the voice.

I fuck her mouth as gently as I can.

The voice is a cruel motherfucker. *If I shock her while you're doing this, she will bite down.*

I fuck her mouth harder. *Good boy.*

I'm close. *Take the blindfold off and come in her eyes.*

"No!" I growl. I pull out of her mouth quickly; my cock bounces out from between her lips a fraction of a second before the electric *crack* at her neck comes alive. She screams, falling backward. The back of her head hits the concrete floor with a sickening thwack, and for a moment I think she might actually be dead. I stand over her still form and watch her chest, making sure it still rises and falls. Her nipples are pink and raised, and my dick still thinks it's getting a release after being in her mouth. *No.* I'm not even remotely turned on by what I've been forced to do to this poor girl.

Boldly, slowly, she reaches up and lowers her blindfold. It's a risk. That could get another shock for her disobedience.

"Why are you doing this?" she asks me.

"If I don't do it, he'll kill you," I say. "Don't make him angry."

"Make who angry?" she asks, her voice trembling, her entire being trembling with fear. She thinks I am a monster. And I am, in some ways, a monster, but I wish she could know that I have no control over what's happening right now.

Last chance, the voice says. *You don't want to ignore me. Take her ass as punishment to you both.*

I crouch at her feet and gather her ankles in my hands, intending to turn her over on to her stomach. *Don't*, the voice says. *You should look into her eyes while you're tearing her apart.*

Terror rises in my throat. I don't want to hurt her – but I don't have a choice. I push her legs wide and she barely resists, staring up at the ceiling; I think, compared to making her choke on me or the electric shocks, sex isn't so brutal. At least, that's what I tell myself as I put my fingers to the tight bud of her asshole.

She jerks away from my touch as apologies fall from my lips. "I'm sorry," I say. She's crying. "Please," she says, trying desperately to wriggle her hips away. "Not there. Anywhere but there."

Her ass is so tight I can barely push my finger past the tight ring of muscle at her entrance. I'm quite sure she's never been fucked here before, and that makes it all the worse. Yet another thing I will take from her as she begs me not to.

I reach up to her mouth on impulse and stick two fingers in, making a scooping motion. I cut her tongue deeply with the rose thorn; the blood is still flowing freely. I take as much blood and saliva from her mouth as I can and spread it around her asshole. Then I press my dick against her tight opening and spear into her in one swift movement that drags a scream from her so horrific, it brings a lump to my throat. I look down to where our bodies are joined – where mine has violated hers – and through the painful squeeze of her tight ass around my cock, I see fresh blood. I have torn into her, ripped her flesh, and I wish so badly that it didn't have to be this way.

Now cut her. With what? I don't have a knife. A weapon of any kind.

With the thorns. Of course.

Listlessly, I reach for the long-stemmed rose and press it down against her forearm. She's already in so much pain, she barely notices when it breaks skin.

More.

Goddamn it. I find another piece of flesh and press, waiting for fresh blood to well up.

More!

I mark her arms and her breasts with the rose thorns before he makes me start on her face. This is our punishment because I refused to ejaculate into her eyes. I should have just done what he said, because now she will be scarred forever. Blood springs up on her cheeks, among the delicate skin around her eyes, across her lips, and I just want this to be over.

Good, the voice says. *This is very good.*

She's crying, her head to the side and her eyes blank and unseeing as she makes little gasping sounds. I want her to feel better. I want to take her pain away. With one hand on the floor to support myself as I push in and out of her, I use my other hand to stroke the tiny bud of nerve endings beneath her barely-there pubic hair. I press my thumb against her clit and rub shallow circles, noticing the way she first constricts around me, and then relaxes fractionally.

"You should come," I say to her. "It will hurt less."

She doesn't answer me or even acknowledge what I've said, but after a few minutes of fucking her ass and stimulating her clitoris, she tightens up around me, her eyes flutter, and I hope she gets at least one small moment of peace among this hell we're in together.

"Have you always heard voices?" she asks me later. After I was done and she'd passed out, I took the new blindfold and a little of the water from the bottle and cleaned her face up as best as I could. I hope I didn't leave lasting scars on her flesh. She's beautiful, and she should stay beautiful, not be marked and disfigured by a psychopath with a fucking rose thorn and time to kill.

"No," I say sharply. Defensively. "Of course not. I'm not crazy. It's—"

A high-pitched sound screams in my head. I hold both of my hands over my ears as a growl wells up from my throat unbidden; at the same time, the girl screams in pain as *crack-crack-crack* the electric collar around her neck springs to life. She's still sitting; her eyes wide, her fingertips up at her collar. This shock was just a warning. A warning to not talk about the voice.

"I'm sorry," I say to her. "I wish I could tell you everything."

She just watches me from her corner; her knees huddled to her chest.

I want to rip this collar from her throat and rub my fingertips across the raw skin where the two metal prongs rest; they have to hurt her.

"When are you going to kill me?" she asks.

Don't answer that, the voice instructs me.

So I don't. I just stare at her, wishing things were different, knowing that they'll only get worse before the end.

There is a girl sitting in front of me. A beautiful girl. I don't know her name, or her age, or what she loves or who she aches for; but I know her better than anyone has ever known her. I don't want to kill her. But after I'm through with her, after the voice is finally sated and lets me rest, I'll definitely kill myself.

Lili St. Germain is the *USA Today* bestselling author of the *Gypsy Brothers* series and the *Cartel* trilogy.

The excerpt above, featuring Rome and Avery, is taken from a brand new dark romantic thriller series that will be releasing in 2017. The **CALIFORNIA BLOOD** series, set in the criminal underbelly of San Francisco, follows two warring families who are ruled by blood, power and twisted desire.

Verona Blood is the first book in the series.

VERONA BLOOD

Avery Capulet is missing.
Taken by a madman. Kept in the dark.
She might not survive.
He'll use her body. Destroy her mind.
All before he even lays a hand on her.
Rome Montague is a drug dealer. A criminal. A thief.
Rome Montague is missing – but nobody will miss him.

Not that it matters; after the things he's done to this girl, *he doesn't deserve to be found.*

For CALIFORNIA BLOOD pre-order links and more, visit www.lilisaintgermain.com/CaliforniaBlood

If you can't wait that long for Lili's new book to release, check out her GYPSY BROTHERS series for the villain readers LOVE to hate! The Gypsy Brothers series centres on a young woman and her quest for revenge, as she infiltrates the biker club who murdered her father and left her for dead. Love, lust and vengeance all collide when Juliette Portland sets out to destroy those who wronged her.

Thank You

Shari, Lili, T.M., Callie and Skye thank you for downloading and reading this exclusive collection. We hope you're not too shattered after finishing - just shattered enough :)

We'll each be emailing you with exciting news on the characters featured in My Sweet Villaintine, plus other upcoming works, specials, author events, giveaways and any other cool stuff we'd love to share with you. If you don't hear from us, please check your junk or spam filters - sometimes our dark treats get caught by email filters!

If you have a friend with a heart full of darkness, please share the link to this collection with them!

The link again is: www.mysweetvillain.com

Now that you've seen in to the darkest recesses of our writer minds, you might also like to find out more about us. You can read up on each author by visiting the My Sweet Villain website and scrolling to the author section.

Until we meet again (in the dark, of course!),

Your Villainesses
Shari Slade
T.M. Frazier
Skye Warren
Callie Hart
Lili St. Germain

LILI ST. GERMAIN

Lili is a *USA Today* bestselling author who has sold over a million books since January 2014. After the success of her self-published Gypsy Brothers series, she was approached by HarperCollins Publishers, who signed her CARTEL series in a three-book deal. The Gypsy Brothers series focuses on a morally bankrupt biker gang and the girl who seeks her vengeance upon them. The Cartel series is a trilogy of full-length novels that explores the beginnings of the club.

Lili is also the author of psychological thriller *Gun Shy* and the *California Blood* series.

Aside from writing, her other loves in life include her gorgeous husband and beautiful daughter, good coffee, Tarantino movies and spending hours on Instagram. She loves to read almost as much as she loves to write.

You can follow her at www.lilisaintgermain.com

SHARI SLADE

Shari Slade is the USA Today bestselling author of sexy new adult romance, best known for her gritty and heart-pounding Devils Host MC series.

When she isn't toiling away in the non-profit sector, she's writing gritty stories about identity and people who make terrible choices in the name of love (or lust). Somehow, it all works out in the end.

Frequently found in a blanket fort, you can also find her at www.ShariSlade.com

CALLIE HART

Callie Hart is the *USA Today* bestselling author of the Blood & Roses Series, the Chaos and Ruin series, and the Dead Man's Ink series. There are few real saints and sinners in her books; more often, the denizens of her stories are all very human. Broken, flawed, and always with the potential for redemption.

She is also busily penning the first part of the New Orleans Nights series, Road to Ruin, which will be released in 2017.

If you'd like to learn more about Callie's books, make sure to follow her at www.calliehart.com

SKYE WARREN

Skye Warren is the New York Times bestselling author of contemporary romances such as the Chicago Underground series. Her books have been featured in Jezebel, Buzzfeed, USA Today Happily Ever After, Glamour, and Elle Magazine. She makes her home in Texas with her loving family, two sweet dogs, and one evil cat.

Her newest books, The Pawn, The Knight and The Castle, are all part of her Endgame series – an addictive dark romance.

When she's not writing about Gabriel Miller and his fictional friends, you can find her at www.skyewarren.com

T.M. FRAZIER

T.M. Frazier is a USA TODAY BESTSELLING AUTHOR best known for her KING SERIES. She was born on Long Island, NY. When she was eight years old she moved with her mom, dad, and older sister to sunny Southwest Florida where she still lives today with her husband and daughter.

Throughout the years T.M. never gave up the dream of writing and with her husband's encouragement, and a lot of sleepless nights, she realized her dream and released her first novel, The Dark Light of Day, in 2013.

She hit the USA TODAY bestsellers list for the first time with Tyrant in 2015 and the fifth book in the KING SERIES, Preppy Part One, was a 2016 Goodreads Choice Awards finalist for best romance.

You can find her at www.TMFrazierBooks.com

Thank you for reading *My Sweet Villaintine*. To keep up to date with the Villainesses check out www.MySweetVillain.com

Printed in Great Britain
by Amazon